BERTIE
and the
BIG RED BALL

BERYL COOK
& Edward Lucie-Smith

John Murray
Gallery Five

For Alexa

The first thing Bertie did when he came to visit Auntie
Ruby at the seaside was to eat the cat's dinner.

'Oh dear,' said Ruby, looking down at the empty
bowl, 'how could I have forgotten to feed poor Mumtaz?'

Mumtaz glared at Bertie from the top of the kitchen
cupboard and said nothing.

The second thing Bertie did when he was at Auntie Ruby's was to go into the back garden and say hello to the tortoises.

'That black dog's a lot too quick for us,' they said to themselves, and pulled in their heads and feet. Bertie tried to turn them over to make them come out and play.

'Oh dear,' said Ruby once again when she came out and found him, 'perhaps I'd better take him for a walk.' Bertie rushed in from the garden and headed for the front door, but then stopped in his tracks in front of the hall cupboard.

'What do you want?' Ruby asked him. Then of course she remembered . . .

She opened the cupboard door, bent over with a big sigh, and rootled around.

'Not that!' she said, throwing out a pair of shoes. 'Nor that,' – it was a hat she'd once worn to a wedding. 'Nor those,' – her old pair of winter gloves. 'Nor even that,' – a basket with a broken handle. 'And certainly not those,' – a pair of giant false teeth she had bought at a local jumble sale, thinking they might come in useful.

'Ah, there it is at last – your big red ball!'

'Yes – yes!' he barked. 'Yes – yes!'

The big red ball was the thing he liked best in all the world. When Bertie had his ball he didn't stop for anything or anyone.

Ruby wouldn't let Bertie off his lead until they got to the seafront. It was a lovely day – the grass was green, the breeze was blowing, and the sea was full of yachts so far away and tiny that they looked like paper boats floating on a pond.

Bertie didn't notice any of these things. All he saw was that big red ball. 'Throw the ball!' he barked. 'Please, please, please!'

So Ruby took a deep breath – swelled up until she almost burst – and *threw it*.

Away went the ball, and away went Bertie after it. It bounced across the grass, and on to a stretch of tarmac where some girls were roller-skating. Bertie hit it with his head and sent it *crash* through the middle of them.

'Oh dear,' said Ruby for a third time. 'All those poor girls seem to have fallen over. Well, if they're no good at roller-skating. I suppose they shouldn't try it.'

When Ruby looked round, Bertie had disappeared. But as she peered into the distance she just caught sight of him vanishing into a big building.

'Oh dear,' she said, 'Oh *dear*.'

Inside something strange was going on. There were a lot of men with big muscles, wearing very small bathing suits. They were standing in line on a stage, making their muscles ripple. Above them hung a banner which said

MR TARZAN BODYBUILDING CONTEST

Bertie didn't have time to read it. He jumped at the ball, and *bump!* suddenly all the musclemen were sitting on their bottoms, looking rather foolish.

'Well Tarzans ought to know how to look after themselves,' said Ruby, when she arrived a moment later. The Tarzans didn't like to argue, since Ruby was bigger than any of them.

'Where's that bad dog now?' muttered
Ruby, standing on tiptoe and shading her eyes
with her hand. Once again she couldn't spot
Bertie anywhere, though away in the distance
she could see a lot of cross-looking people
waving their arms.

She decided to pretend for a moment that
Bertie and his ball were nothing to do with
her. She put her hands behind her back and
tried to whistle. The noise she made didn't
sound very convincing.

Bertie meanwhile was halfway down the road into town. Right in the narrowest part he met a policeman.

'Stop at once!' shouted the policeman. 'Dogs who chase balls in the street are a danger to traffic!'

Ruby arrived just in time to help the policeman to his feet and rescue his helmet. But then she saw Bertie disappearing into the distance, so she began to run after him. Since she was wearing high heels, it made her ankles wobble.

Away went the ball and away went Bertie after it. The ball bounced into a pub with Bertie in hot pursuit. Ruby stood outside, wondering what to do. From inside came a terrible clucking and squawking. It sounded like hens waking up in a henhouse.

Suddenly Bertie and his ball and three fat ladies were all trying to get through the doorway at the same time. One of the fat ladies was clutching an umbrella. She brought it down with a great *whack*, just missing Bertie, but hitting another fat lady on the shins, who howled and hobbled away.

Meanwhile Bertie had bounced his ball
right into the middle of the fish-market.

A live crab got Bertie by one of his paws.

'*Ow-Ow-Ouch!*' cried Bertie as the crab
pinched him, and he jumped straight through
the front window of a nearby Fish Restaurant.

There was a terrible crash of breaking glass.

When Ruby arrived, Bertie had just escaped by the back door and they were clearing up the mess. There seemed to be soup everywhere – even in the owner's beard.

'Never mind, love,' he told Ruby. 'We can always make some more. That crab your dog left behind will make lovely soup. Join us tonight for a double helping.'

Bertie had lost his ball and was looking everywhere for it. He came to a big road where a Royal Marine band was marching proudly along. At any other time Bertie would have stopped to enjoy the music, but suddenly he saw the ball just in their path. So he tapped it with his nose . . .

Now it was getting dark, and Ruby still couldn't find Bertie. She'd gone back to the seafront to have one last look for him. Away out to sea the big red moon was rising.

All at once the moon began to bounce. It came closer and closer and grew bigger and bigger.

'That's not the moon at all,' cried Ruby. 'That's a big ball, and Bertie's still chasing it. *Something AWFUL's going to happen !*'

'Oh dear,' said Auntie Ruby, waking with a start on the sofa, where she'd just stretched herself out for forty winks before they left, 'what a strange dream'. And there's poor Bertie, waiting patiently for his walk. 'Shall we go up on the seafront then Bertie, and take that big red ball with us? You know how much you like to chase it.'

'Yes-yes!' barked Bertie, rushing first to the cupboard and then to the front door. 'Yes-yes! YES-YES!'

Beryl Cook's paintings are sold in London through Portal Gallery Ltd

Limited edition prints of some of Beryl Cook's paintings
are available from The Alexander Gallery, Bristol

Greetings cards and prints of many of Beryl Cook's paintings
are available from Gallery Five Ltd, London

Design by Ian Craig

First published 1982
by John Murray (Publishers) Ltd, 50 Albemarle Street, London WIX 4BD
and Gallery Five Ltd, 14 Ogle Street, London WIP 7LG

Printed in Italy by New Interlitho SpA

British Library Cataloguing in Publication Data
Lucie-Smith, Edward
    Bertie and the big red ball.
    I. Title   II. Cook, Beryl.
    823'.914[J]   PZ7
    ISBN 0-7195-3976-5

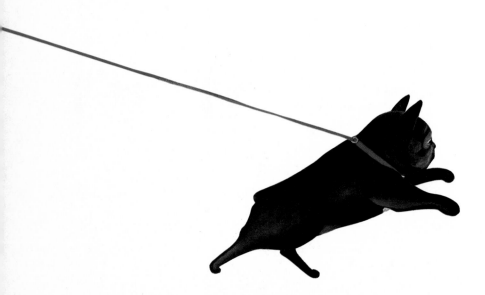